D1545000

Lonely Veronica

written and illustrated by

ROGER DUVOISIN

Lonely Veronica

EVANSTON PUBLIC LIBRARY
CHILDREN'S DEPARTMENT
1703 ORRINGTON AVENUE
EVANSTON, ILLINOIS 60201

x D
cop. 7

Bs1072516

Alfred A. Knopf  **New York**

L. C. catalog card number: 63-14603

THIS IS A BORZOI BOOK, PUBLISHED BY ALFRED A. KNOPF, INC.

Copyright © 1963 by Roger Duvoisin

All rights reserved. No part of this book may be reproduced in any form without permission in writing from the publisher, except by a reviewer, who may quote brief passages and reproduce not more than three illustrations in a review to be printed in a magazine or newspaper. Manufactured in the United States of America, and distributed by Random House, Inc. Published simultaneously in Toronto, Canada, by Random House of Canada, Limited.

Text set in Bodoni Book. Composed at Westcott and Thomson, Philadelphia, Pa. Printed by Reehl Litho, New York City.

Veronica's river was so slow and lazy . . . It looked like a green snake asleep in the grass. It was so quiet . . . the old trees on its banks were reflected on its waters as in a mirror.

Ripples and waves broke the image of the trees only when Veronica and the other hippopotamuses dived and splashed, for food and for play. And only the songs of birds or the cries of wild beasts broke the silence of the sleepy river's shores.

It was a peaceful, contented river, with happy hippopotamuses.

Then, one day, men came.

They did not walk, like good hippopotamuses. They rode big machines that roared and smoked like a forest fire. The old trees that stood in their path came crashing down in tangles. The forest became a desert of mud and dead trees.

"It's the end of the world!" cried the hippopotamuses.

Men had come to build a big highway and a city on the shores of the peaceful river, and a bridge to cross over it.

The hippopotamuses held a council, and everyone gave his opinion amidst the roars, the smoke, and the dust. But in the end, the elders spoke:

"We can see that the good old days here are gone. We must leave our forefathers' river to search for another quiet river, far from men and their hubbub."

So they led their herd away through the forest.

But Veronica remained. She thought, "Old hippopotamuses always speak of forefathers and good old days. *I* am a *young* hippopotamus. I want to see the good *new* days."

She went up the river bank to watch the cranes, the bulldozers, the steam shovels, and the dump trucks dance like giant beetles amidst dead trees, holes, and piles of dirt.

"Look who comes here," shouted a bulldozer driver. "VERONICA."

"Good day, Veronica," said Joe, the foreman of the machine crew. "I like your smile, Veronica. But don't go too near the machines."

"Ha, ha, I have an idea," cried a gentleman in a jeep. "Veronica, you will be the first guest in our new city's zoo."

A little square house was built for Veronica, with a little square yard and a little square pool, and she watched the world from behind iron bars.

That is how Veronica began her life in the good new days.

Veronica was not sure whether there was reason to rejoice or to cry over the change in her life. But Joe the foreman knew.

"Veronica," he said, "you have lost your lovely smile. It is clear you are not happy. But do not worry. My crew and I have come from across the sea to help build the new city. We are going home now. Come with us and be the pet of the machine crew."

That explains why, on a hot morning, Veronica was swung high up by the crane of a big steamship, only to be lowered into the hold onto a bed of fresh palm leaves. She was soon on her way to America.

What a sight awaited Veronica when the crane lifted her out of the ship. All around was the biggest jungle she had ever seen. A jungle of square houses, some small, some fat, some taller than the tallest jungle trees. And all those noises! And all those busy little men!

"Ah," smiled Veronica as she dangled on top of the crane. "I wish those old hippopotamuses could see me now!"

Every morning in the big city, Joe and his crew took Veronica on the dump truck so she could watch the bulldozers, the cranes, and the steam shovels push, pull, dig, build, and demolish.

"Look, Veronica," cried Joe. "Look how we demolish this big, tall house so we can build an even taller one in its place."

Veronica saw the big house come down, bing, bang. She saw it carried away bit by bit in dump trucks. She saw a hole dug deep into the earth where the house stood—so deep that she became dizzy looking down into it, and rolled right down the big planks upon which the trucks carried the earth away.

"Watch out," cried Joe, running after her. "There goes Veronica."

"Oh, well," said Veronica trying to smile at the bottom of the hole. "That's nothing. Hippopotamuses' skins are thick. Just right for rolling into holes."

But she *was* full of bumps and bruises which Joe and his crew patched up.

Now Veronica watched the bigger house fill up the hole again. She watched it grow out of the hole. Grow up, up, up, into a tall tower, through the clouds, to the sky.

"It must be nice," thought Veronica one late Friday afternoon, "to go up in that big box which carries Joe, and other people, and things, to the top of the tower."

She went into the box. No one saw her.

As she turned around, her tail hit the starter and zoom . . . the box went on its way, to the sky.

So while Joe searched for Veronica at the bottom of the tower, Veronica peered down into the city from the top. But as she found now, one can get even dizzier looking down into a big city than into a hole.

"Hooooooooo," gasped Veronica, pulling back. "OOOOOHHH," and her legs wobbled. She crawled back into the box and waited for it to go down. But the longer she waited the less the box seemed to want to go down.

Night came. The millions of little windows became lamps which lighted up the city. It was beautiful. But Veronica was asleep.

When dawn awoke Veronica, the city was sunk into deep fog. Only the top of the tower stood out like an island in the sea. Here, there, and far away, other tower tops were like sister islands.

Everything was so still. Veronica was so lonely. "More lonely," she said to herself, "than I ever was in my jungle. More lost. More hungry."

But now, looking about the floor, Veronica saw some stairs which went down. Men's stairs, of course. Men never think of hippopotamuses when they build stairs in tall towers.

Veronica tried to go down
backward . . . forward . . .
sideward . . . one step, two
steps, three. She slipped,
stopped, and finally rolled
down onto the floor below.

Since the stairs went on down, Veronica tried again. Now on her back, now on her stomach, sideways and all sort of ways. One step, two, three, four. Then she slid down on her back to the next floor.

Veronica remained on her back for a while to rest and to think of other ways hippopotamuses could go down men's stairs. "I think there just isn't any other way," she said. So she crawled, rolled, and crept down more steps. At midday she was so weary and hungry she lay down to sleep.

But suddenly she was awakened by the *coo-coo-cooo* of a grey pigeon who alighted at her feet. "I could not believe my eyes from afar," said the pigeon, "but there you are, a HIPPOPOTAMUS above the clouds!"

"Yes," moaned Veronica, "here I am. You don't have to tell me. Rather tell me, little pigeon, how one climbs down tall towers. And how one eats in them."

"Well, one *flies* down. Easy," answered the pigeon. "And one can eat in towers as everywhere. On sidewalks, on window sills, on roofs . . . one just looks. Of course, one must be a pigeon. But pardon me, I haven't introduced myself: ALEXANDER."

"Veronica," said Veronica.

"Where do you come from, Veronica?"

"From the good old days in the forest by the hippopotamus river," murmured Veronica in a dreamy voice.

"Never heard of it. *I* come from the ferry dock by the river. Now, Veronica, I saw that two floors below here somebody left a few sandwiches, three apples, and lots of lettuce leaves. And a pail of water. Meet me there and we will picnic together."

The pigeon flew down and when Veronica arrived he exclaimed, "Heavens, how long you have been. I thought you had fallen asleep."

"Alexander," asked Veronica, swallowing three apples, "do you know how many more steps there are to the bottom of the tower?"

"Lots more than I can count, Veronica. But I dare say, at the speed you go it will take you two more days to get there."

"Two more days? With only those crumbs to eat? But I'll starve! No offense to you, of course, Alexander."

"Don't mind me, Veronica. If I were a lone hippopotamus in a tower I would worry too. Because, you know, workmen won't come to help you tomorrow, it's Sunday—or the day after; it's a holiday. But pardon me if I hurry off. I have many things to attend to."

All afternoon Veronica crawled, crept, and plodded down steps. She was starved, bruised, and glum that night when she collapsed on the floor to sleep. In the morning, two half loaves of bread and two bananas, which dropped on her nose from a hole in the ceiling, woke her up. It was Alexander who had pushed these things through the hole.

"How you worried me, Veronica," said Alexander. "You are now so deep inside the fog I couldn't find you. Didn't I tell you one can always find one's meal in the city?"

"So could I in the jungle," sighed Veronica. "And a HIPPOPOTAMUS's meals."

"Possibly," said Alexander. "And *I* would starve there. Maybe."

"Alexander, how many more steps are left? I can't see with the fog."

"Lots, lots, lots, Veronica. So you had better start crawling down. Bye-bye now. It's a busy day for me."

So again Veronica crawled down steps, slept here and there to rest, and crawled. All day long.

The next morning Alexander alighted on Veronica's nose with noisy flutters of his wings.

"VERONICA, WAKE UP! Don't you know you have been sleeping on the street floor? Three cheers, Veronica!"

But Veronica was too weary to cheer. She only sighed a long, long sigh. Besides, there was no reason to cheer, yet. The bottom part of the tower was already enclosed with walls and all the openings had been closed with boards for the long holiday.

"*That,*" muttered Alexander, "is something I never, but never, thought of. And I can't think of what to do!"

"I shall sleep," groaned Veronica. "Sleep, while you fly off to attend to your affairs." So Veronica slept, the rest of the day and through the night. She dreamed she was splashing in the hippopotamus river and eating mountains of delicious water plants.

She was awakened by many hands which petted her on all sides, and by many voices saying, "VERONICA! Here is Veronica! We have found Veronica!"

"Dear Veronica," Joe was saying, "wake up. How tired and thin you look. And to think that we searched for you all over the city. Why, were you here all this time?"

Beasts cannot tell their secrets to men, so Joe never knew. But Veronica smiled because Joe was with her at last.

"Veronica," said Joe now, "I must tell you what I thought while we looked for you. What is there for a hippopotamus to do in the world of men? The zoo? The circus? Watching bulldozers demolish things forever and ever? No, no, not for our Veronica. I am going to take you to my father's farm far, far out in the country. My father has asked me to find a pet for his grandchildren. And I thought—what nicer pet can there be for children than sweet Veronica?"

Veronica's eyes twinkled with joy. She even found strength to get up.

"And Veronica," Joe went on, "during my vacations, you and I will lie in the grass together, by the pond under the old oak trees. No hubbub, no machines, no crowds of people. Just like the good old days!"

"Hi, Veronica," cooed Alexander, who had flown in. "And I'll visit you too. These will really be the good *new* days for you."

"You know, Alexander," said Veronica with the happiest of smiles, "I think there are no good *old* days; there are no good *new* days. There only bad and good days."

So Veronica went away to the country where she lived very, very many good days under the old oak trees by the clear pond, often in company with Joe and Alexander.

EVANSTON PUBLIC LIBRARY
CHILDRENS DEPARTMENT
1703 ORRINGTON AVENUE
EVANSTON, ILLINOIS 60201